The First Day at High School:
A smile for Karen Amanda

EUGENIO MIGUEL DEDIEGO

All rights reserved. The total or partial reproduction of this work is not allowed, nor its incorporation into a computer system, or its transmission in any form or by any means (electronic, mechanical, photocopying, recording, or otherwise) without the prior written permission of the copyright holder is a violation of these rights and may constitute a crime against intellectual property.

The content of this work is the responsibility of the author and does not necessarily reflect the views of the publishing house. All texts and images were provided by the author, who is solely responsible for their rights.

Published by Ibukku, LLC
www.ibukku.com
Cover Design: Ángel Flores Guerra Bistrain
Grpahic Design and Layout: Diana Patricia González Juárez
Copyright. © 2024 Eugenio Miguel Dediego
ISBN Paperback: 979-8-89727-069-9
ISBN eBook: 979-8-89727-070-5

"To my daughters, Karen and Cata"

Karen Amanda sleeps soundly while Grandpa Lorenzo dozes off, letting a thin trail of drool escape from his mouth and fall onto the arm he rests on the rocking chair. Between his legs, he holds the old storybook he reads to Karen Amanda every night before she sleeps. The room is small, cluttered with multicolored toys scattered everywhere. A rag doll seems to cling to one of the legs of the simple bed where she naps. A gust of wind bursts into the room with force, making Grandpa cough. He shifts in the rocking chair, trying to stand, but he can't, and the book slips from his hands, landing on the floor. He glances at Karen Amanda, who barely stirs, stretching one leg.

"I think it's time", he murmurs to himself as he tucks her in. He kisses her forehead and leaves the room, heading to his own. The moonlight floods her room with a soft glow as Grandpa's weary figure enters his own. Kneeling by the edge of the bed, he pulls out a medium-sized chest. The lid is adorned with carvings of faces Oof aborigines laughing, astonished, shouting, joyful, grumpy, and more. He opens the chest, and a light beams from inside, casting its rays into the four corners of the room. From within, he takes out two objects wrapped in gift paper. Standing up, he pushes the chest back under the bed with his foot.

Grandpa walks slowly, carrying the two gifts in his wrinkled hands. He pauses at the doorway of his daughter Carmenza's room. He notices her sobbing but feels relieved when he realizes the cause is the soap opera she watches every night at this hour, where a woman endures the humiliations of an unfaithful husband. The television rests atop a large dresser, sharing the space with jars of cream, perfumes, makeup items, and small cardboard boxes. Grandpa enters and kisses her on the forehead, wishing her goodnight. She responds absentmindedly, not wanting to miss a moment of the show.

"The mighty dragon breathes bursts of fire, and the villagers flee in fear. Karen Amanda stands in the beast's path." She stirs in her bed, dreaming of the story Grandpa had told her earlier. At that moment, he enters her room and gently places the two gifts into her warm hands. Then, he sits in the rocking chair beside her bed, opens the storybook on his lap, and smiles. The wind grows fiercer, sending warm gusts that rustle the book's pages. The lights flicker, and Grandpa lowers his head, gazing at Karen Amanda. And there, surrounded by silent witnesses, the toys, the heroes on the posters lining the walls, the rag dolls, Grandpa Lorenzo takes his final breath.

The light of a new day filters in from every corner, illuminating the modest home of the López family. Karen Amanda opens her dark eyes, her beautiful face lighting up with life. She clutches the gifts tightly in her hands and becomes alarmed when she sees Grandpa Lorenzo still in the rocking chair.

She sets the gifts down on the bed. Her worry eases when she notices a smile on the old man's face. The pink giraffes and elephants on her pajamas seem eager to find out what's going on with Grandpa. She approaches him and gives his shoulder a little shake.

"Grandpa! Grandpa, wake up!"

But Grandpa doesn't wake. So, she turns her attention to the card attached to the gifts.

"FOR MY KAREN… FROM YOUR GRANDPA." She clutches the gift wrap tightly, trying to tear it, but the paper won't give. She rummages through a drawer, finds a pair of scissors, and tries cutting it, but the paper is as tough as a sheet of steel. Defeated, she decides to slide the gifts under her bed and runs out of the room, calling for her mother, who is in the kitchen preparing breakfast.

"Mommy! Mommy! Grandpa won't wake up… come, let's go to my room," the little girl shouts to her mother, who hurries to see what's happening.

"What do you mean he won't wake up, huh?" her mother asks as they enter Karen Amanda's room. Her mother's eyes fill with tears, and a faint rainbow appears, caused by the light reflecting off her eyelids.

"Why are you crying, Mommy?" Karen Amanda asks, rubbing her hands against her pajama. Her mother moves toward Grandpa, gently removing the storybook from his lap.

"Grandpa has passed away, my love," she says, sobbing. She searches for a blanket adorned with suns and moons from Karen Amanda's bedding drawer. Karen Amanda remains still, quietly observing Grandpa.

Nervously, she exclaims: "But he's smiling, Mommy!"

"It's just the expression on his face; he seems happy, but he's gone" her mother replies, now somewhat calmer. Karen Amanda hugs her mother, and they cry together. They leave the room slowly, leaving the blanket on the bed. "If Grandpa goes to heaven, will we be alone, Mommy?" the girl says through sobs.

"Your Grandpa is now with the angels... I'll take care of you and read you the stories... Grandpa will be watching over us." Her mother wipes the child's tears and then, seated in the small living room, picks up the phone to make arrangements for Grandpa's funeral. A cold wind moves through the tubular furniture, brushes past the small telephone table, and hits the wall. Her mother is lost in thought. "Your first day of school will have to wait; I need to handle all the funeral details." But the girl doesn't hear her; she's already back in the room, looking at Grandpa. Karen Amanda feels a strange sensation of joy, followed by a calmness that relaxes her. Suddenly, an image of her grandfather speaking to her appears before her eyes. "You're going to be an excellent graduate, my Karona" comes the voice of an emotional Grandpa, his face filled with love.

"But I won't be able to share it with you, Grandpa" the girl says sadly.

"It was time for me to leave... My body was very tired. But I will always be with you, my spirit! Never forget that, and never doubt it" he assures her, as his image begins to fade. The girl tries to hold onto it, but she cannot.

Only the smile seems to remain on Grandpa's face. The girl picks up the storybook from the table and places it back on the old man's lap. She then searches under the bed for the gifts and puts them into her school bag, along with her new notebooks, each marked in her Grandpa's handwriting. She takes one and studies the letters carefully. Her Grandpa's voice speaks again:

"Don't be sad, my Karona, I'll always be with you."

The girl wipes away her tears, and at that moment, her mother enters.

"You shouldn't be here. Let's go, my child! Grandpa needs to rest in peace." The girl looks at Grandpa's smile, while her mother sees only a lifeless body and covers him with the blanket. They leave the room, hugging each other.

Don Lorenzo was buried in one of the city's two cemeteries on a rainy, dreary afternoon. Karen Amanda and her mother returned to their small house, which now felt lonelier than ever.

On a clear night, when a vast full moon filled the sky and its light streamed through Karen's window, her mother tried to read her a story from the book. But it was useless, for the sadness gripping the child's heart consumed her completely.

"And the prince was unsure… to kiss her or not… What to do?" her mother says enthusiastically, as the girl lets out a yawn. "You don't want to know what happened with the prince, do you, my dear?" her mother asks, and the girl shakes her head. "I already explained it to you. After the funeral, Grandpa went to heaven" she says, somewhat irritated.

"But why did they put him in that box?" the girl asks, sucking her thumb.

"Well… they put his body there, but his soul…" her mother replies, now calmer.

"It left his body."

"But why did he have to die?" the girl says, raising her voice.

Her mother brings her fingers to her head and scratches it, trying to find the right words to answer her daughter's question.

"I know Grandpa was very special to you, but things can't change now" she says, feeling a bit confused.

The girl gazes at a photograph on the table, showing her mother, herself, and Grandpa.

"He said he would never leave me" the girl says, tearfully.

Karen Amanda is deeply sad and melancholic. Her days turn into a monotonous routine, where she has abandoned her rag dolls to a bag; the storybook lies on a small table, now like a cold stone, gathering a layer of dust. She no longer watches TV as she used to. She locks herself in her room, and the laughter that once filled it seems to have gone off to find other children.

Her mother grows increasingly worried, fearing that Karen's mood could make her ill. Both are seated having breakfast, and her mother feels excited about Karen Amanda's first day of school, hoping it will help her recover and move past this bitter time they're experiencing.

"Do you want more juice, honey?" Mother asks cheerfully, with a smile.

"No, I don't want any more."

Karen eats without enthusiasm. The sliced bread with jam, the guava juice, and the eggs all taste bland to her, like nothing at all. She imagines Grandpa sitting with them at the table.

Her mother smiles nervously and says:

"You'll see, you're going to make lots of friends. There are so many kids at that school; they must play all the time! … Are you listening to me, Karen?"

"Yes, yes, I'm listening." Half-distracted, she checks that the gifts are still in her school bag, while her mother tries to make light conversation.

"And what about your lunchbox, huh?"

"You know you don't bring a lunchbox to high school."

"That's true, my little high schooler!"

They fall silent and finish their breakfast. The mother remains thoughtful while Karen gets up and heads to the bathroom, where she brushes her teeth in front of the mirror. A few minutes later, she hears her mother's voice.

"Hurry up, my love! We're going to be late for school."

***

In the Eternal Games Park, children of all colors play forever, without the presence of adults. They play marbles, top spinning, mother and father games, and coca, etc. These children radiate happiness from every pore, and their toys change into an endless variety of bright colors. However, the presence of a strange old woman signals the end of joy and fun. Shadow has transformed into this old woman, dressed in gray, wearing leather sandals, and with a wart on her nose. She carries a basket containing green mangoes with salt, which she offers to the children. She walks hunched over, supported by a dry, thick branch.

"Mangoes! Mangoes with salt! Free! Free!" The old woman shouts as she approaches twin girls, who stand out for their skill at playing marbles. The old woman blows a dark breath over the mangoes, making them glow intensely.

"These will be the Earthquakes" the evil old woman murmurs to herself. The children stop playing and gather around the woman. "These are special, my favorites, for you" she says, pulling out a pair of mangoes and offering them to the twins.

"How delicious!" Says the light-skinned twin, savoring it as she bites into the fruit.

The dark-skinned twin frowns and says:

"Umm! More salt, please."

"Of course, they're tasty, aren't they?" The children nod quickly, moving their heads up and down and wide-eyed. The mangoes, covered in salt, pass from hand to hand, and when it seems like there are none left, the old woman shakes her basket, and they multiply. She places it on the ground, and the children push each other, eager to eat another mango. The old woman, without hurry, moves away from them. Her wrinkled face reflects the malevolent intent she holds. It is then that, behind a nearby bush, she throws the dry branch, which turns back into a snake, slithering away and disappearing. The shadow leaves the old woman's body in the form of thick, dark smoke, which rises and vanishes from the place. All that remains of the old woman are a few mounds of ash.

"What happened to the old lady?" Asks the dark-skinned twin while savoring the salt on her fingers.

"She left, and we didn't even thank her" says the light-skinned twin, shouting aggressively, her eyes lost.

"Let's play!"

The basket is left battered, forgotten beside the drawn game of marbles.

The children resume their games, with the bitter taste of the mangoes in their mouths and a growing sensation of nausea and pain in their hearts, under a sky turning gray.

***

The large building stands imposing, with its balconies and windows facing the street.

Three floors of knowledge, made of concrete and finished with fine wood; a large guayacán gate, with carvings and inscriptions, serves as a backdrop for Karen Amanda to say goodbye to her mother, who accompanies her to the entrance of the school. Karen wears a pink jumper, white blouse, and tights, with burgundy moccasins. Her mother sobs and kisses her on the cheek.

"My girl, before we know it, you'll be a young lady. Imagine, you'll be in high school soon" her mother says, while Karen's heart beats faster at the new experience she is about to start. "Look, you can buy something at break time" she says, more cheerfully, as she hands Karen a bill.

"It's not break; it's rest. If you say "break" here, they'll call you a schoolgirl."

Most of the children have already entered the school.

Karen is one of the last to arrive, and the institution, represented by a teacher, has given her special waiting time.

"Don't forget, classroom 6-A. You'll introduce yourself to Miss Liliana Torres, a blonde with blue eyes."

"Kind of crazy, on the first floor" the girl replies. "How many times are you going to tell me?"

"I'll ask for permission at the office and come pick you up after school."

"Yes, Mommy. Don't worry."

"And put on a better face, my love."

Her mother blesses her with her right hand and watches as she enters the building. She wipes away a tear that escapes down her cheek. Karen Amanda disappears behind the heavy door.

Karen Amanda approaches classroom 6-A. The door is open, and she steps in silently.

"Good evening, Karen Amanda" says Miss Liliana with an ironic tone, remarking on her lateness.

Karen Amanda, backpack on her shoulders, stops and looks for an empty seat.

"Sit over there, next to the saints" the teacher says dryly.

Karen Amanda sits beside the twins —one dark-skinned, the other light— who greet her with hostility, sticking out their tongues and rolling their eyes at her.

"Boo! Booooo!" the twins hiss. The teacher shoots them a look, and they fall silent.

Karen Amanda takes off her backpack and sits where the teacher directed her.

"Alright, let's continue the lesson... Now, where were we...?"

A bell rings three times, its sound reaching every corner of the school, followed by the chaos of students pouring out of their classrooms for a short break. Karen Amanda feels lost in the crowd; overwhelmed and confused, she follows a group of girls to the bathroom. With her backpack still on, she locks herself in one of the stalls. The bell rings again, and the students return to their classrooms, not even noticing the absence of their new classmate.

Karen Amanda sits on the bathroom floor, opens her backpack, and takes out one of the two unopened gifts. She tries to tear the wrapping paper and, to her surprise, it gives way easily, revealing the elongated figure of a smiling pencil.

"Hello! How are you?" the smiling pencil says to the girl. She startles and drops it.

"Careful, please! I could break... My tip is very sharp."

Karen Amanda examines it from head to toe. The talking pencil has two legs, two arms, white gloves, and a yellow body. On its head, a red eraser. Its face has bulged eyes and a fixed, cheerful grin.

"How can you talk?" The girl asks, frightened.

"I don't know, but I enjoy it. Didn't your grandfather tell you anything?"

"He never mentioned you" she says, a little calmer.

"Well, let me tell you, my dear Karona. My name is Piloso."

"How do you know my name?"

Piloso, pretending to be in pain, exclaims:

"Your grandfather marked your notebooks with my blood! Oh, what a tragedy! Ahhh! I know many things about you, and I can do many things for you."

Piloso stretches his body and peeks over the bathroom stall door, which was slowly closing.

"The coast is clear. You can come out now, little one."

"Who said I want to come out?"

Piloso shrinks back to his normal size and draws a roll of toilet paper, which materializes as he hands it to Karen Amanda.

"Thanks, but I don't need it."

"No problem, I'll erase it" says Piloso, extending his red eraser to make the paper disappear.

"No, leave it here, please. Another girl might need it."

"A thousand things I can draw, stretch out far or shrink so small, face wild beasts or hide away... That's me, Super Pilosín, yeah!" Piloso sings excitedly.

"Well, I don't know what I'd need a gift like you for. Maybe to do my homework."

Piloso moves as if dancing; he shakes his hands, takes light jumps, and his ever-smiling face seems full of life.

"The old man told me that homework is your responsibility alone."

"Well, I don't want to know anything or learn anything at all. I don't like this school. I want to leave... and you, Pilosín, get in the backpack because I'm out of here" says Karen Amanda. Frustrated, she shows Piloso the backpack and immediately opens the bathroom door.

"I can get you out of here, but you have to ask properly" no shouting and with moderation.

Karen Amanda pulls a lever, flushing the toilet.

"No! Not that way!" Piloso cries out in terror.

"Please, help me get out of here."

Piloso is moved by Karen Amanda's plea. Without hesitation, he draws a hole in the air, right at the height of the girl's head. In the center of the hole, a swirling vortex of water appears, but upon closer look, it is actually images moving at an incredible speed. A small ladder extends from the hole, and Piloso gestures for the girl to follow him. She adjusts her backpack and slings it over her shoulders.

"This way is much better than that one" he says, pointing at the toilet.

Karen Amanda follows Piloso as he climbs the ladder. Finally, both disappear through the opening, which seals itself in midair, while the toilet water returns to its normal level.

Karen Amanda and Piloso reappear near the Park of Eternal Games, where children are playing. The girl is thrilled by the sight of their apparent joy, but as she tries to step forward, she nearly falls into an abyss. Piloso, now the same size as Karen Amanda after stretching himself, grabs her arm just in time.

"Whoa! That was close. Piloso, can you help me, please?" She pleads.

"To make you smile again, I'd do anything, anything at all!"

"Then bring my grandfather back" she says wistfully.

Piloso remains silent. Both stare into the abyss, which is deep but narrow, from which toxic gases and intense heat rise. Then, with a serious tone, Piloso says:

"I can't do that. The dead must be left in peace."

His voice soon regains its cheerful tone.

"But this abyss, I can control it."

Immediately, Piloso lies down on the edge of the abyss, stretching his body, though still not reaching the other side. Karen Amanda steps onto the improvised bridge, but as she reaches the end, she hesitates.

"To move forward, you must trust that you won't fall."

Calm and fearless, Karen Amanda keeps walking. Piloso stretches further, supporting each of her steps, until she safely crosses the abyss, letting out a sigh of relief.

"Always trust yourself, and you will achieve anything" says Piloso as he shrinks back to his normal size, and she places him inside her backpack. At last, Karen Amanda is close to the children.

"Can I play? Please?" She asks, pleading with the girls playing hopscotch, who seem to be in a foul mood.

"Wait your turn!" Shouts the fair-skinned twin, while the dark-skinned twin gets ready to take her turn. "It's my turn!" She growls, jumping onto the first square of the hopscotch game. The moment her feet touch the ground, the earth trembles. Karen Amanda drops her backpack, scattering her notebooks, the gift, and Piloso onto the dirt floor.

"Be careful! Don't jump so hard… Why is everyone eating green mangoes?" Karen Amanda asks, at this, the fair-skinned twin growls, stomping her feet in frustration, causing more tremors and powerful waves that send the children playing marbles flying into the air. Their betting money gets caught in a whirlwind. Those arguing while playing house are also shaken by the twin's tantrum.

"What was that?" Asks the father.

"Don't change the subject, young man" snaps the mother aggressively.

"But… don't you see how everything is shaking?"

"So what? Let it shake all it wants, that doesn't change how irresponsible you are."

"And? That's why I'm the one with the money, ha!"

The father throws the plates, pretending to eat, onto the ground, and the mother bursts into tears.

Some children fume with anger because their marbles have become too heavy to lift; the tops refuse to spin, no matter how much string they wind around them. Karen Amanda and Piloso, recovering from their fall, watch the chaos unfold as the children struggle to control their endless games.

Karen Amanda insists once more, with a quiet:

"Please, can I play?"

The twins nod.

Everyone watches in anticipation, eager to see what will happen. Karen Amanda tosses a marker and jumps onto the first hopscotch square. Nothing happens. The absence of any tremor mixes with the relieved sighs of the children, who had feared an even bigger quake.

"Stop playing. It's for the best, you won't have any more problems that way" says Piloso, stretching and shrinking his body while fixing his slightly disheveled face.

"No, Piloso, playing is the best thing… We children need to play a lot… Life is playing and playing."

"Yes, my Karona, but here, it seems to be the opposite."

The children continue playing, aggressive, ill-tempered, and the earth keeps trembling. Piloso wanders around and discovers the basket of mangoes. Karen Amanda stands deep in thought.

"Look what's here!" Exclaims Piloso, his eyes widening in astonishment.

Karen Amanda examines the remaining mangoes in the basket and, with certainty, says:

"These mangoes are rotten… This must be it. Everyone is eating these contaminated mangoes. Some children are still consuming the green mangoes, though they are no longer quite green but rather dark and foul-smelling."

Meanwhile, in front of the BullFrog family's cabin, Shadow transforms into a baby of that frog species and begins crying at the top of its lungs. Mrs. BullFrog, who is pregnant, opens the door. Her golden horns gleam as she appears, wearing a camouflage apron over a wide red dress. Seeing the baby, she feels compassion and picks it up. The baby does not stop crying:

"Muuubrooomuuu! Brooobrooo!"

"Oh, what an adorable little baby! Oh! What beautiful eyes! Agu! Agugu!" Mrs. BullFrog is too emotional to see beyond appearances; those eyes only reflect an inner chaos.

Mrs. BullFrog cradles the baby in her hooves and heads toward the corral, where her husband, Dr. BullFrog, is having fun being chased by his flying green cape. She watches as his red horns try to catch it. He is wearing a sleeveless camouflage coat, left unbuttoned, and short blue pants. As she approaches with the baby, who had started to calm down, it suddenly begins crying again.

"You scared him. I'd better make him a bottle... He must be hungry." Dr. BullFrog is surprised and stops charging at the cape, but his wife has already turned back toward the cabin. She enters the kitchen, places the baby in a basket, and prepares the bottle. She grabs a tin labeled: "SAPOLTECA MILK, THE BEST."

"I'm going to make you a super-vitaminized, delicious bottle. You'll see!"

She hums a lullaby while preparing the bottle, but the baby is anything but sweet; its aggressive eyes measure the extent of the destruction it plans to cause.

***

In the park of the Eternal Games, Karen Amanda finally discovers the cause of the children's aggression and bad temper. She opens a mango, and a swarm of tiny black worms wriggles out.

"Ew! Gross! ... I got it, Piloso! Draw me some cotton candy clouds, please."

"And what for, my Karona? Are you planning to make it rain sweets?"

"You'll see. Trust me" she says with confidence.

Immediately, Piloso draws fluffy clouds of cotton candy in multiple colors and sizes. Karen Amanda takes a piece and offers it to one of the twins.

"Look at this delicious cloud" Karen Amanda says kindly.

"Why would I eat something like that?" The twin asks aggressively.

"I'll trade it for your mango… And it's free!" Karen Amanda insists.

Upon hearing the word "free," the twin agrees to the exchange. She takes a bite of the cotton candy cloud, and a smile spreads across her face.

"It worked! It worked, Piloso! Help me give some to all the kids, and you too!" she says to the now-smiling twin.

"What happened?" Asks the dark twin, confused.

"Don't worry, everything's fine" Karen Amanda reassures her.

All the children eat from the cotton candy clouds. The effect is instant: they become kind again, their laughter fills the park, and they resume their games without any trouble.

"If it worked on these kids, maybe it will work on you too; you could get your smile back! Try it!" Piloso suggests.

Karen Amanda eats an entire cotton candy cloud.

"It's useless. I don't feel anything" she says melancholically.

"Let's play with the kids… Maybe that'll cheer you up."

"Let's go!"

They go through every game, participating and being welcomed as just another pair of children. But eventually, Karen Amanda grows tired and decides it's time to leave.

She grabs her satchel, bids farewell to the children, and, accompanied by Piloso, departs. They exit the park, approach the abyss, which immediately seals itself, and continue on their way.

The girl and the talking pencil walk along a dry, dusty, stone-covered path, flanked by withered pines. They hum a tune together.

"As I walked along one day, I went! I went!"

"I went! I went! I went!" Piloso chimes in.

"When suddenly, a frog jumped out! Croak! Croak! Croak!"

"Croak! Croak! Croak!"

A man appears on the path, riding a motorcycle equipped with two enormous speakers blaring at full volume, drowning out Karen Amanda's song.

They watch as the medals on the man's jacket glimmer with tiny flashing lights as he approaches.

"What a racket! You'd think it was a party!" Karen Amanda complains.

The noise grows even louder. The man adjusts his sports cap and pants, then grabs a microphone.

"Ladies and gentlemen..."

Immediately, a chorus of coordinated laughter is heard.

"Hee, hee, hee! Ha, ha, ha! Ho, ho, ho!"

"It can't be! Again, once more" the man laments as he dismounts from his motorcycle and introduces himself:

"I'm General Star." He shows off his bright white teeth. "Yes, sir, that's me. Expert in conflicts, social relations; advisor to the most powerful, and not because I'm needy..."

He pulls out a list of diplomas from his motorcycle, connected by a plastic strip, and they fall to the ground. "I'm educated, yes indeed! I've got diplomas even from the International Diploma Organization; I can even catch a lightning bolt by its tail! That's me!" He puffs up his chest with pride.

"You sure know a lot, General Star... And those laughs... They seemed like mockery" the girl comments.

"What can I say, my dear... Let's take it step by step. First off, I'm not a "don," I feel old. Take away the "don." And what's your name?"

"Karen Amanda... I called you "don" because you inspire respect... But the laughs..."

"And this charming little friend here" says the general, avoiding the girl's question. He hands them his personal business cards.

"My name is Piloso, yes sir! That's me!" Piloso says proudly.

"Karen Amanda, is that your name? Do you know anything about repairs?... It's related to the laughs."

"What laughs?" The girl emphasizes.

"It's my audience. They've always cheered me on, applauded me, but lately all I hear are these fake laughs" the general says, sounding somewhat nostalgic.

"Tell me, what's going on?" The girl asks, moved.

The general Star tries to speak into the microphone, but the laughs drown him out. Through the speakers, a chorus is heard:

"Ha, ha, ha! Hee, hee, hee! Ho, ho, ho!"

"General, please, talk to me about your speech... And put down that microphone" the girl says.

Piloso begins to examine the motorcycle closely. A strong wind lifts dry leaves and twigs into the air, while they cover their eyes.

"I like the microphone... I always begin with a loud "Ladies and gentlemen," then I talk about pain, tragedy, the plan to improve, the new taxes for creation, the friends to be named, and so on, until I finish, and I don't know why they start crying."

"And still asking why" Piloso responds, wiping away his tears.

"I think you should start by greeting everyone, not just the ladies and gentlemen. Talk about nice things, and don't shout" the girl interrupts.

"That's it! I have a brilliant idea!" Says General Star excitedly. He opens a small door on one of the speakers, and a crowd of people fills a square.

"I ask for just one opportunity, just one... I know my mistakes, and I want you to listen to me this time" the general says pleadingly to the crowd, which settles on benches, in the shade of the trees, some with pocket radios, all eagerly awaiting. They can be seen through the speaker's small door. Piloso dilates his eyes as if to hear the general better. The girl winks at him, symbolizing victory with her fingers and wishing the general success. He returns the gesture and takes the microphone, which seems about to fly away from the nervousness of the speaker.

"Good... good day, my beautiful people, life colleagues, joyful children, cool grandparents, loving parents, enthusiastic youths, all my people. We are one blood, one heart, a people of successes, here the creators fight for it, we build hope every day."

The general's eyes sparkle like gold nuggets amidst the confusion that seems to possess him, but a sudden downpour of applause and cheers erupts from the crowd, stunning even the most distracted. The general turns off the microphone and excitedly approaches the girl.

"Thank you, Karen Amanda; I am so grateful. I needed the oxygen of applause, the sap of cheers."

"I come from a lineage doomed to applause; without applause and cheers, I would never be happy."

"It feels so good to feel like this!" The girl says, with a melancholic tone.

"As thanks, let me accompany you. Where are you headed, on this dry path?"

"To happiness" Piloso responds.

"Ah! Happiness! You're close."

The general whistles a tune as they continue their journey. They march on, escorted by the general, until the path splits. He raises his hand to say goodbye, accelerates his motorcycle, and disappears in a cloud of dust.

"What about the general, huh?" Piloso says, ironically.

"He's got a great sound system."

"He could be president!" Piloso jokes. Karen Amanda disapproves with a look on her face. Piloso gets scared and says: "Could he?"

They walk a few more meters in silence. Nearby bushes rustle, and a whirlwind of leaves rises into the air. They stand still, expectantly, waiting to see what happens next.

The baby BullFrog enters the laboratory, destroying several of Dr. BullFrog's utensils and potions before releasing a foul breath and exiting. The doctor arrives, a few minutes later, at the door of his workspace and surveys the scene of destruction.

"My formula! My formula!" Shouted the doctor, frantically searching among the shards of broken flasks and spilled liquids. Mrs. BullFrog rushed in.

"What is this? What happened?"

"Where is the baby?" Demanded the doctor aggressively.

"You can't possibly think that such a sweet little baby did this!"

"He's the only visitor we've had in years."

"I'll go look for him." She hurried off. She searched the rooms, the kitchen, the pen, but couldn't find him. Her bulging eyes filled with tears; she simply couldn't believe the baby could have caused such destruction in the laboratory.

The BullFrog baby, his eyes wild and drooling, entered the lagoon, contaminating the water, turning it viscous, blackish, and foul-smelling. Shadow abandoned the baby's body and drifted away from the BullFrog family's lagoon.

The doctor rushed out, reached the shore, and was hit by the putrid stench of the lagoon.

"Croak! Croak! Croak!" He bellowed, his powerful croak echoing into the darkening sky.

The echo of his croak was heard by Karen Amanda and Piloso, who were frozen in fear at the sudden appearance of the Blue Dragon from behind some bushes. They saw the reflection of light shimmering off the beast's blue scales as it blocked their path.

"Oh no! It's him! It's him!" Cried Karen Amanda, slightly terrified.

"Whoever he is, he's getting ready to roast us."

"It's the Blue Dragon from the story!"

"Well, you're going to introduce me to him now," said Piloso as he stepped protectively in front of the girl.

"Open the gift! Open the gift!"

"Which one!?"

"It's in the bag!" Both of them stepped back as the menacing beast advanced.

"It's him! Such a beautiful blue!" The girl pulled out the gift her grandfather had given her, unwrapped it, and out came a ring the size of her head, with a dark area in the center.

"What is this?" She asked, intrigued.

"It's a portable hole. Throw it near the dragon and command it to open," answered Piloso. "The Blue Dragon! Throw it! Throw it, Karona!" shouted Piloso in distress.

The Blue Dragon prepared for a second attack, gathering an even larger blast of fire. The girl threw the portable hole at the beast's feet.

"Open!" She commanded as she stepped back.

At that very moment, the beast lunged forward to attack, and the hole opened, swallowing the dragon whole as it fell into its own flames.

"Close!" The girl commanded as she stepped forward and picked up the hole, from which a faint wisp of smoke escaped, as if the flame of a torch had been plunged into water. Once again, the echo carried the sound of a croak to them.

"And that sound... What happened to the Blue Dragon?"

"Dragon roast. Just kidding, Karona. You only sent him to another story... As for that sound, I have no idea what it could be," joked Piloso.

"Thank God nothing happened to him. I like reading about the Blue Dragon's adventures," said the girl, carefully placing the portable hole back in her bag.

"Take good care of it. It works really well... and best of all, it doesn't talk."

"How big can it open?"

"Oh! A lot. Once, in a travelers' tale, it swallowed an entire cruise ship."

"I was so close to the dragon," said the girl, amazed.

"Close to being his dinner," Piloso pointed out.

They both continued down the path, drawn toward the sound of the croaking, which grew louder with every step. They passed through a small forest and from there caught sight of the lagoon and the BullFrog family's cabin. As they approached, the cabin seemed strangely enormous.

Karen Amanda asked Piloso for a ladder, and he stretched his body up to a window. The girl climbed onto him and peered inside, watching Dr. BullFrog pacing back and forth, examining something under his microscope and snorting furiously.

"It can't be! Two hundred years of research lost in a single minute. It can't be!" he muttered angrily to himself.

"What can't be?" The girl interrupted from the window.

"And what are you doing up there, climbing like that?" the doctor demanded aggressively.

"I'm sorry for arriving like this," the girl replied, embarrassed.

Suddenly, the doctor's sticky tongue shot out and grabbed the girl by the hair.

"Ow! That hurts! That hurts!"

Mrs. BullFrog hurried in, despite her pregnancy. Piloso, alarmed, quickly drew a pair of scissors, ready to cut the doctor's tongue.

"Let her go! Let her go, please!" Pleaded Mrs. BullFrog, and at her insistence, the doctor released the girl.

"You shouldn't be spying through windows... That girl could bring us more trouble," the doctor grumbled.

"She might also bring something good. Don't be so distressed," his wife reassured him as she embraced him. "The babies will be fine," she added, touching her swollen belly.

While they exchanged opinions, Karen Amanda and Piloso reached the door. The doctor remained in the laboratory, and Mrs. BullFrog invited them into the kitchen, where wooden shelves were filled with provisions that only this kind of family would eat: beetle bonbons, sugarcane worms, butterfly jelly, canned sweet worms, canned cricket legs...

"Forgive my husband, but he is very upset."

"Please forgive me instead. I shouldn't have spied; that's what doors are for."

"For spying," joked Piloso.

"No. For knocking on," the girl insisted.

"But you're such a lovely girl. What are you doing so far from home?"

"Thank you for calling me lovely. We are on our way to happiness. That's our path... And forgive me for asking, but when are you expecting the baby... I mean, the babies?" The girl inquired, glancing at Mrs. BullFrog's belly.

"I don't know exactly, but it won't be long now... And you, what are you doing with those scissors?"

"I use them to... to cut my nails or maybe to clip the horns off an unfaithful person... You know... 'putting horns'..." Piloso answered, somewhat uncomfortable.

Mrs. BullFrog moves around the kitchen in silence, arranging utensils and making sure the cookies in the oven didn't burn. The cookies were shaped like various insects.

"But what's the problem? Your babies will have a beautiful home, just like this one," the girl broke the silence.

"The problem is the lagoon."

"They're delicious…"

"Well… I'll pass. Thanks," said Piloso.

Karen Amanda eagerly ate the cookies but quickly calmed down as the doctor entered the kitchen.

"I'm sorry, sir," the girl spoke nervously.

"Do you see a 'sir' here? It's Dr. BullFrog to you! … And you, what were you planning to do with those scissors?" He said, turning to Piloso.

"To cut… my nails. Or, you know, just in case someone tries to put horns on me," Piloso replied, taking off his white glove, revealing enormous nails, and glancing at the doctor's horns.

"Look at this girl… Don't you think she's lovely? They're heading toward happiness," Mrs. BullFrog intervened.

"She is a girl with a pure heart… Forgive me for being rude to you."

"You don't need to apologize, Doctor. How can we clean the lagoon for the babies?"

The doctor grabbed a few cookies from the tray with his sticky tongue and exclaimed:

"There is a bigger problem. Let's go to the laboratory, please."

"Go to the laboratory while I prepare a special dish-garlic-fried flies, with a dessert of tender grass," said Mrs. BullFrog. Upon hearing this, Piloso's eyes widened in shock at the special meal.

They entered the laboratory. Dr. BullFrog frantically searched for something amid the mess. The micro-watershed was in ecological imbalance, and it required a girl with a pure heart to smile and descend into it to restore equilibrium.

"The micro-watershed is disturbed. The wolf aged too quickly from eating contaminated fish and can no longer chase the hares."

"The hares are multiplying, eating too many plants, and eroding the land. Everyone is starving! Obviously," the girl interrupted the doctor.

"It's the wolf's fault! He should change his diet!" Piloso joked.

"Here it is. This is it," the doctor said, taking a small vial between his hooves, where the colors of the rainbow swirled back and forth.

"With this, you'll smile. I guarantee it. You will be happy," the doctor said as he sprinkled part of the vial's contents over Karen Amanda. Immediately, she began to smile, then burst into uncontrollable laughter.

"Ha, ha, ha! And they're starving! Ha, ha, ha! The hares! Ju, ju, ju! They eat so much!" The girl laughed while Piloso took the opportunity to draw happy faces, hopeful faces, faces of celebration. But suddenly, she started to cry.

"Poor little fish! Poor things!" The girl sobbed.

"I think the potion has also been affected," the doctor concluded. He whistled, and the green flying cape wiggled its ends, swiftly soaring from the corral to the laboratory. The doctor made a signal with his hoof, and the flying cape wrapped around the girl, spinning her around.

"What happened to me?" The girl asked as she regained her senses.

"You were smiling, just how I want to see you! But then you started crying," Piloso replied, taking a deep breath and looking around aimlessly.

"Doctor, may I look at the micro-watershed?" The girl asked, still somewhat confused.

"It won't be a pleasant sight," the doctor warned as he adjusted the microscope for her. She peered into the device and felt a pang of sorrow upon seeing the old wolf's face. His sad eyes seemed on the verge of tears as he looked back at her.

And in a forest clearing, Shadow, in the form of a dark cloud, invokes the ferocious wolf to stop Karen Amanda.

"I summon you, beast of calamity, and through what I provoke, I see you arrive." The voice sounded hoarse, and a whirlwind of dirt and dry leaves swirled, forming a vortex at its center. A wolf appeared, the grinding of its fangs echoing through the air. Shadow cast its energy onto the wolf and commanded:

"Here, motionless, you will wait for a girl who will pass along this path."

The ferocious wolf was instantly paralyzed, its gaze fixed on the road, while Shadow evaporated and vanished.

Meanwhile, in the laboratory, Karen Amanda burst into tears upon seeing the wolf's tragic expression. One of her tears fell into the micro-watershed, triggering a heavy downpour. The doctor hurried to observe through the microscope, as the girl could no longer bear to look.

"The contamination is beginning to fade! The wolf looks strong and rejuvenated!" The doctor shouted excitedly.

"How could this be?" Karen Amanda sobbed.

The doctor, holding a test tube in his hand, said:

"Give me one of those tears, and I'll explain."

He collected a few tears rolling down the girl's face and began hopping joyfully on his long frog legs. The commotion in the laboratory caught the attention of Mrs. BullFrog, who quickly arrived.

"And what's this celebration about? What's happening?"

The doctor embraced and kissed her before replying:

"The micro-watershed contamination is gone, thanks to the girl's tear falling into it!"

"They must be very sweet tears, and one dropped into the micro-watershed. Maybe you eat a lot of sweets?" Piloso joked.

"And for the lagoon... the babies will need it soon," Mrs. BullFrog interrupted, looking concerned.

"Don't worry! These tears are miraculous! Let's go outside!" The doctor reassured her, holding up the test tube.

Everyone hurried out of the cabin and rushed to the edge of the lagoon. Dr. BullFrog poured the test tube's contents, letting the tears drip one by one into the vast, foul-smelling water. Gradually, the murky liquid cleared until it became intensely crystalline.

"Look! Look! What a marvel!" The doctor gestured.

"Can we go swimming now, doctor?" Piloso asked.

"Do as you please... I don't know how to thank you, child."

"I didn't do anything, I just started crying."

"Thank you, Karona, you don't know how much you've helped our species," Mrs. BullFrog interrupted.

"I'm Karen Amanda, who called me Karona?"

Both looked at Piloso, who pretended not to notice. Meanwhile, the doctor removed a thick whistle from around his neck and handed it to the girl. She accepted it with excitement.

"Thank you... but it doesn't make a sound," she said after blowing into it.

"You must blow while thinking of someone, and only that person will hear you. But be careful: if you blow softly, it will be pleasant; if you blow hard, it will hurt," the doctor explained.

Karen Amanda thought of her mother and blew gently. In her office, her mother paused from her routine, gazing at a photograph of her father, her daughter, and herself. Then, for no apparent reason, she felt a sense of calm before returning to her typewriter.

"I hope she heard me," the girl sighed.

"She did, rest assured... We're leaving now, Karona. And you, best of luck with the eighty babies," Piloso said as he bid farewell.

"It's not that many, maybe fifty, and most will survive," Mrs. BullFrog clarified.

"We're going to repopulate this lagoon... and the entire valley. It's been a long time since our species has reproduced... A thousand thanks."

"Once they're fertilized, take good care of them," the girl advised.

"Why don't you stay for dinner?" Mrs. BullFrog suggested.

"No, ma'am, thank you, but we must leave now!"

They enthusiastically said their goodbyes and resumed their journey, leaving behind the cabin by the lagoon in the valley.

The sky over Numberland, made up of numbers and mathematical symbols, began to darken with a spreading black stain, sending its inhabitants into panic.

"Kalkuleitor! Kalkuleitor!" Shouted the terrified numbers and symbols.

"Kalkuleitor! Kalkuleitor!"

An elderly man, slightly hunched over, with glasses and disheveled hair, wearing a shirt and pants decorated with formulas, equations, and symbols, appeared. He was Kalkuleitor, and he barely had time to glance at the sky before becoming paralyzed. Instantly, the numbers and symbols that had been running across a grid-like floor also turned to stone.

Everything remained motionless. At that moment, Shadow materialized into a beautiful woman, draped in delicate silks, her hair cascading down to her waist, her eyes clear and piercing. She snapped her fingers, and Kalkuleitor started moving again, followed by the numbers and symbols. Shadow walked gracefully toward Kalkuleitor, whose heartbeat was the only sound that could be heard, pounding as if it were about to leap from his chest. She stopped in front of him, right at the entrance to the school palace, where an inscription above the door read: "GIVE NUMBERS A HEART." The numbers and symbols held their breath.

She took him in her arms, tilted him back, and kissed him passionately. He transformed into a muscular man, now wearing dark sunglasses and a tuxedo, but with a heart that barely beat. A bitter melody spread through Numberland, throwing its numbers and symbols into chaos.

***

The fierce wolf's restless eyes seemed ready to jump out of their sockets when he spotted Karen Amanda and Piloso walking along the forest path. The beast shook off its frozen state, ready to devour them. The girl sensed the danger and, slightly frightened, spoke:

"I feel like we've met before. What are you doing around here?"

"I'm waiting for some friends of mine..."

The wolf circled around them; suddenly, his ears grew disproportionately large, and Piloso couldn't hold back his laughter.

"What big ears you have!" Piloso teased.

"They're for... they're for flying better," the fierce wolf muttered, revealing his sharp fangs. The girl, now a bit calmer despite the wolf's threatening claws, intervened:

"Are you, by any chance, looking for the three little pigs?"

The wolf grabbed his head with his claws and shook in frustration.

"Don't try to trick me, little girl."

"You're the one getting tangled up, like a passion fruit vine. Now you want to be Dumbo, thinking you can fly with those little ears?" Piloso said sarcastically.

The wolf's ears shrank back to their normal size as the two cautiously kept their distance. The fierce wolf made a few aggressive movements in the air, then suddenly started rapping while moving his claws. With a rhythmic flow, the beast rapped out his confusion:

"I don't know where I belong, in this path I walk along,

Do I wait for a girl, or chase the pigs I've known so long?

Or maybe in a cottage, there's a grandma all alone,

Or the boy who loves to lie, crying wolf with every tone!

"The wolf! The wolf! The wolf is here! Awooo!"

He tricks and he tricks, spreading fear everywhere.

I don't know where I belong, between these paths I roam.

But girl, don't try to fool me—

'Cause I just might eat you whole! Awooo!"

The wolf used his rap to distract them and prepared to attack, but the two were already on guard. The girl threw the portable hole at him, commanding it to open. The wolf leapt, dodging it, baring his fangs.

"What a big mouth you have!" Shouted Piloso.

"It's to devour you!" The wolf retorted, circling them.

"Pilo! A net, please!" The girl asked, frightened. Piloso soared up and began drawing the character Maya the Bee from a comic strip, but quickly erased it after seeing the girl's disapproving face. He finally drew a net that fell over the wolf. He apologized to the girl, who was excited to see the wolf trapped.

"Bravo! Bravo!"

"Not so fast, little girl," the wolf's voice was heard as it slashed through the net with a swipe of its paw.

"Shoot its legs, the legs, please!" The girl pleaded anxiously, grabbing the whistle. Piloso shot a stream of glue at the wolf's legs, making them stick to the ground. The girl blew the whistle thinking of the wolf, and it howled in pain. Piloso prepared by stretching the eraser's rubber and threatened the wolf.

"I'm going to erase you from the map, little wolf."

The girl stopped blowing, and the wolf kept howling. She asked Piloso not to do anything to it, since the wolf couldn't defend itself, pinned to the dirt floor.

"But, Karona, we can't leave it here… someone could come along, and this wolf would cause trouble."

The girl approached the wolf and spoke to it, asking it to promise to behave in exchange for its release. The fierce wolf whimpered and promised to be good, but immediately its ears grew back to an enormous size.

"You must promise it with the heart of a dancing wolf," the girl said.

"With the heart of a white fang, a police dog's heart, Lassie's, whichever you want, I promise!" the wolf replied, distressed, and its ears returned to their normal size. The girl was convinced by the wolf's sincerity and asked Piloso to set it free.

"Alright, my Karona, all for the little wolf to walk the path of good."

Then, Piloso shot water at the wolf's legs and freed them. The fierce wolf wagged its tail, shook its paws, and attacked again.

The girl reacted and blew the whistle so hard that the wolf felt its eyes almost pop out. It kneeled and begged:

"I beg you, little girl, please don't blow anymore. I'll behave."

Piloso drew a book and made the fierce wolf swear an oath.

"Come on, put your paw here... By the way, I congratulate you, you rap very well."

"Now you want to hear me again?"

"No, leave it for later… now swear, this is the sacred book of wolfdom; from your ancestors," Piloso said, while Karen Amanda reminded the wolf of the importance and seriousness of the moment. The wolf swore confidently.

"I swear to behave from now on."

"Take the book with you; it'll help when you feel tempted."

"Now you can go. When in doubt, don't forget about me, and I'll blow! And I'll blow!" the girl informed him, holding the whistle near her mouth. The wolf left, and when they no longer saw him, the girl blew the whistle softly, thinking of him. Then, they heard his howl.

"That wolf had it fierce," said Piloso, smiling.

"It's better to let it go ahead… How much longer until happiness?"

"I can't tell you how much longer, that's something only you will discover."

They walk slowly and then decide to sit on something that looks like a log. The girl taps on this surface.

"I'm afraid I won't find it," she says, a bit sad. They both look at each other when they feel the supposed log move. The girl taps again, and suddenly, a centipede starts running. They, feeling the rough surface beneath them, jump off.

"What a scare!" The girl sighs.

"How exciting!" Piloso exclaims, then notices a girl in a red hood with a basket, walking along the path. She approaches, and Piloso asks:

"Where are you going?"

"I'm going to my grandmother's house to bring her these peach palms."

"Peach palms! I love peach palms!" Karen Amanda interrupts, savoring the thought.

"Well, here, take some... I'm in a hurry!"

"If you run into a wolf along the way, say hi from me."

"And what's your name?"

"I'm Karen Amanda, but tell him that the girl with the whistle remembers him... Thanks for the peach palms."

"Tell him we're watching him," Piloso intervenes while the girl continues on her way.

Karen Amanda enjoys eating the peach palms and soon falls into a deep sleep.

"Wake up! Wake up! We need to keep going," Piloso says, alarmed, but the girl doesn't react.

The voice of the grandfather reaches the girl's dream for the first time.

"Wake up, you must continue searching for happiness. It's not time to sleep! It's time to dream! Wake up now!"

The girl jumps up from the dirt floor and, feeling very encouraged, says:

"We must keep going."

"Yes! That's it, let's go now!"

***

The imposing school palace appears, its facade decorated with countless formulas, symbols, instructions, etc., in front of which Karen Amanda stands with her mouth open, astonished at all the unknowns. They both realize the injustice of the even numbers —strong and powerful— oppressing the odd numbers, weak and languid, subjecting them to harsh trials, making them pay high percentages, while they live very well.

Piloso and Karen enter the palace and walk down a hallway made of fine hypotenuses, which leads them to a spacious hall. There, a chubby eight is whispering into the ear of the great Kalkuleitor, waiting for his wise counsel, while beside the throne, from their school cage, the symbols of Addition, Subtraction, Multiplication, and Division shout for freedom.

"Yes, that's how it should be. The answer is simple, divide and you'll get more profit... Who's next?"

A cylinder approaches, pushing a languid seven.

"I, sir! Look at this repeat offender... He was supposed to give us seven percent and only gave us five."

"What?! You shouldn't operate like this... For the next payment, you'll have to work harder and pay nine percent," Kalkuleitor says indignantly.

"Yes, beloved Kalkuleitor," the seven responds fearfully.

Karen Amanda raises her hand and says:

"Sir, I'd like to ask a question."

"Go ahead, ask, I always have the answer."

"Tell me why you have Sum, Rest, Multiply, and Divide imprisoned. It seems to me that you're not operating correctly."

Kalkuleitor falls silent, then looks at the ceiling of the palace, which has a dark, slimy, jelly-like substance on it.

"They're imprisoned because they don't operate correctly. You can ask them." The girl, somewhat distrustful, looks around and approaches the prisoners, who are talking among themselves in an agitated manner.

"Let me ask you, what function do you have?"

The imprisoned symbols go silent for a few seconds. Then they try to answer her, but all that can be heard is a commotion. She intervenes.

"Alright, please, one by one, you start," she says, pointing to Sum, who looks depressed.

"I'm less than nothing, I'm nothing at all." Rest takes the floor, excited, and says loudly:

"But I'm more, I sum everything!"

Piloso approaches Multiply, seeing him very sad, and tries to understand why.

"I feel divided, part of me here, another part there. I don't know how I'll end up.

"You'll end up annihilated, not like me, who feels good when multiplied; profits on the rise, always growing, says Divide, cheerfully.

"What do you think, Pilo? They're really messed up.

"They need a shrink.

"As you can see, if I free them, they will disrupt the kingdom, says Kalkuleitor.

"The kingdom is already disrupted, the girl replies, at this, Kalkuleitor lowers his dark glasses and reveals eyes that look irritated, as if he hadn't slept in the past few days. The girl closely observes the walls and the characters who fill Kalkuleitor's court. A thick, black drop falls onto her blouse, staining it. She looks up at the ceiling, where the dark cloak seems to be boiling. Piloso does the same, but neither of them nor anyone present seems to notice or find a ceiling like that unusual.

"I want to ask you something, and I expect the truth. What's one plus one?

Kalkuleitor pauses, thinking, then starts with a slight smile, which turns into loud laughter. Everyone catches his laughter, except for Karen Amanda, who remains serious, waiting for the answer.

***

At that moment, Shadow looks at Karen Amanda through the mirror-board in Numberland and makes a decision: to alter things in Rosita's garden, where, on the other side of the mirror-board, she is teaching the children in her class. She reaches her hand into the mirror-board, which turns liquid, and pulls out colors, letters, flowers, etc., for the children to learn in that outdoor classroom where the mirror-board floats a meter above the floor.

"Look closely, now I will take out the numbers from one to ten," says Rosita as she reaches her hand into the mirror-board, but no numbers come out.

"How strange! Numberland has never failed me... well, get your fingers ready, let's cut some paper figures."

The children take sheets of paper, and with their fingers in scissor position, they begin cutting flowers, rabbits, apples, crabs, snowmen, cakes, marbles, etc. Then, she invites them to play and sing.

The children begin to fall asleep, while she takes a blanket and covers them. She removes her white coat, her thick glasses, and sits in front of the mirror, which begins to vibrate. A bright light emits, and a handsome prince extends his hand to her. She takes it, and he steps through the mirror.

"Oh! My beloved! I only wished to be by your side. I feel so deeply in love."

"It can't be such beauty. Tell me I'm not dreaming, when I behold such royalty," she says, bringing her hand to her face, a little embarrassed. The prince, kneeling, kisses her hand, and she is already under the sway of Shadow.

"For a long time, I've observed you performing such noble work, and I've become smitten with you; would you, perhaps, give your life the flavor of mine?"

"Yes! Yes! I accept, as long as there is love.

"Then let's seal this union.

The prince lifts her into his arms and kisses her. She falls under his influence, and chaos begins.

"I must go defeat a dragon, as is my duty. Prepare everything, for we will marry when I return.

The prince departs through the mirror-board from which he had emerged, not before casting an evil breath over the children who are still asleep. Rosita mistakes it for a kiss meant for her. The prince walks down a path, his departure watched by Rosita, who gazes at him as he fades from view.

***

Meanwhile, everyone laughs in Numberland at Karen Amanda's question. The laughter fades as they see Kalkuleitor growing increasingly troubled, pondering too much and making conjectures, facing a problem he finds too difficult. Silence falls, and, very proudly, the girl says:

"It's very simple, one plus one is two; logical."

The symbols and numbers cheer wildly, while Kalkuleitor throws off his dark glasses and messes up his hair.

"Triangles! Cancel her! I won't allow such an answer!" Kalkuleitor exclaims angrily, and at his call, a guard of squares rushes in.

"Here's a mistake. These are squares because they have four sides. Please, Pilo, some triangles!" The girl tells Piloso, who immediately draws triangles in the air.

"And these are triangles because they have three sides," she finishes explaining, to the admiration of those present. Sum, Rest, Divide, and Multiply feel much clearer.

Kalkuleitor feels humiliated, unable to bear that a little girl is explaining such simple things to the great Kalkuleitor. All he can do is sit down and start crying. Moved, the girl says to him:

"It's all in the mind," she says and kisses him on the forehead. Suddenly, everything becomes clear for him, transforming him into the bent, gray-haired, gentle old man everyone knows.

"You said it well, symbols and numbers, it's all here," says Kalkuleitor, touching the girl's head as he thinks about logical order. Things begin to resolve in the kingdom, with the even and odd numbers putting aside their disputes. Suddenly, some cubic roots are unearthed from the palace gardens.

"We were convinced we were square... Ah!" Comments one of them.

Sum, Rest, Multiply, and Divide are freed and, together, they begin handing out diplomas, certificates, mentions, and other awards that formed the roof of their school cage.

A soft creaking grows louder, and everyone looks up at the ceiling. The dark, sticky layer had dried and began to peel away slowly until it falls and evaporates before the astonished gaze of the onlookers. Fearing it might crush them, they find the ceiling intact, clean, and shining with a new luster.

"That's the shine of simple things," says Kalkuleitor excitedly, as they all admire the beautiful ceiling.

"Let's give a big round of applause to this lovely girl... Now I decree that we all play, and that everyone needs to relate a bit more to reality," Kalkuleitor encourages the numbers and symbols, who immediately applaud.

"Yes! Because numbers are in everything, even in soup," Piloso says to the girl after hearing the old man.

"What do you mean?" She asks.

"Well, if you're going to make a delicious soup, you need to know how much water you add, how many potatoes you use, how much salt you subtract, how many bowls of soup you divide, and so on."

"Then, let's have more soup!" Comments the girl.

Everyone starts playing and singing. Karen Amanda and Piloso leave, satisfied with their work. They head toward Rosita's Garden, guided by an intense sun that, high above, seems unable to lower the heat of its rays.

"Something tells me we should go to Rosita's Garden," Piloso says, worried.

"And how do we get there?" The girl asks.

"Very easily, we can do it right here."

Piloso draws a board with a mirror on it and steps through it, but the girl can't follow. In her attempt, she collides with her own reflection.

"I knew you could do it!"

The girl shakes her briefcase, adjusts her gardening overalls, and with Piloso by her side, approaches Professor Rosita, who is placing a sign at the regular entrance of the garden. The sign reads: "NEED A TEACHER WHO CAN TEACH HOW TO DREAM WHILE DREAMING." Professor Rosita is wearing overalls, rubber boots, gloves, and holding large scissors.

"Are you here for the vacancy? I'll soon be leaving this job; you see, I'm getting married to a prince," says Rosita kindly while adjusting the sign.

"Congratulations, Professor," the girl says.

"What's your name, little girl?"

"My friend is Piloso, and I'm Karen Amanda."

"Nice to meet you, madame," Piloso says with irony.

"Aren't you a bit too young to be a teacher?"

They walk towards the classroom, where the desks are empty.

"The important thing is that I can fulfill my duties and be responsible," the girl says confidently.

"If that's the case, I'll put you to the test, as an assistant." Rosita confirms the position for the girl, and then, with her scissors, she moves towards the children who are planted in the back of the classroom. Their arms extend into branches, and their feet are firmly rooted to the ground, resembling happiness. Rosita cuts some dry leaves and twigs from them.

"Doesn't it hurt them when you cut their branches?" The girl exclaims, frightened about the fate of the child-tree.

"No, on the contrary, they become more beautiful." The teacher smiles. She walks over to a shelf, sets the scissors down, and gazes at some jars and containers covered in dark mold.

"You need to water them with the Special Water; come, I'll show you how to prepare it."

"I hope it doesn't contain anything that flies or slithers," Piloso jokes.

A murmur rises among the children-trees, which gradually grows louder until Rosita, feeling a bit uncomfortable, lets out a terrible scream. Silence and fear take over the air. The teacher takes a deep breath, trying to calm herself, and explains to the girl how to prepare the Special Water as she gathers what she needs from the shelf.

"In this watering can, it is prepared; to five liters of water, you add five fresh vowels, nine bittersweet numbers, primary colors to give them flavor, one essence of nearness and another of distance. That is all they need to know."

"Is that all? Isn't something missing?" The girl asks in astonishment.

"Yes, I always forget this little bottle... half a teaspoon of Love, stir well, and water their roots... Does it seem difficult? If you accept, you must be very careful with the youngest ones." The teacher places the small bottle on the side of the shelf. Inside that bottle, the colors of love are continuously swirling. They head towards the youngest tree-children, who are planted in small pots.

"You must blend this," says the teacher, tearing some knowledge from a thick book.

"Then, you prepare the bottle," she finishes saying and hands the nourishment to a baby tree, which enjoys it with great satisfaction.

"Everything is very clear," the girl concludes.

"Such bitter things!" Piloso confirms.

"You must be responsible... Children need the basics for their lives... Ah! If you are hungry, heat up some alphabet soup that is in that pot," she says, pointing to a pot covered in soot, and sighing deeply, she adds: "Soon I will marry, oh! My prince charming, when will he come?"

Karen Amanda pretends not to notice. She contemplates a withered tree-child and immediately takes the watering can and applies the Special Water, but the tree-child does not turn green.

"Can you paint it green, please, Piloso?" The girl asks, distressed. Piloso instantly paints it green, but it dries up again. Rosita, who was walking away, notices what has happened, returns, and hands them a bag of plasma on which it reads: "LEARNING ENTERS THROUGH PAIN."

"No problem. Whenever a child dries up, you connect this," Rosita informs her and immediately connects the plasma to the tree-child. The tree-child screams as it feels some letters and numbers enter its body. At last, it calms down, and she disconnects the plasma. Green and a smile return to him.

"How gruesome!" Piloso comments, horrified.

"Are you questioning my method? Every teacher has their own style," Rosita says, upset.

"Forgive him, he is very expressive. And how do you assess the results?" The girl intervenes, managing to calm Rosita down.

"Come with me, some are about to show their results."

They head towards a group of more developed tree-children, who begin to bloom; black flowers, which are Rosita's pride, but from one flower, a white petal blooms. The teacher becomes furious, scolding the tree-child.

"This is what I have taught you. Ungrateful! Inventor! You get a zero chick, insufficient, unmet achievement, failed. There is an error in the answer!" She shouts very angrily, pulling at her white coat, causing the tree-child to burst into tears. The black flowers crumble as she extracts from the mirror-board a sign that says "FAILED" and hangs it on one of the branches.

"So many things have made me hungry; you're in charge, I'll be right back, I'm going to the board, Rosita says to the girl. She then stands in front of the board, from which she pulls out a large red onion." She dedicates herself to biting into it and sighing:

"Loves me! Loves me not!" With each bite she takes of the onion.

Karen Amanda and Piloso waste no time; taking advantage of the opportunity to work without Rosita's presence, they prepare the Special Water again. This time, instead of a teaspoon of love, the girl pours in the entire bottle. They water the roots of the older tree-children and bottle-feed the youngest ones. A few minutes pass, and the tree-children bloom in an explosion of colors. Instantly, their branches and roots disappear, transforming into arms and feet, returning to being normal children, who immediately start playing.

Rosita, with some tears on her face, comes to supervise the work of the new teacher.

"What have you done? So much color, these are not my truths! You have destroyed my years of work, my ideals!" Rosita exclaims in horror.

"I'm very sorry, teacher."

"You're fired, silly girl!"

"If that was just a trial run, imagine being hired! Ah!" Piloso chimes in with a grin.

Rosita collapses onto a wooden chair, which creaks a soft melody, but it is not enough to soothe the teacher, who begins to cry at the sight of the children playing everywhere. She feels as if she might burst with rage. Karen Amanda seizes the moment to serve a glass of Special Water, adding the last remnants of the bottle of love.

"Teacher, drink this, it will calm your nerves," the girl offers to the bewildered woman, who takes the glass and drinks its contents. Seconds pass, and the effect of the drink takes hold. A joy fills her, and she feels love for her children once again. She frees herself from the boots and gloves. She looks for her coat, which has now bloomed. She returns to being the teacher she once was. Turning to the board, she pulls out cakes, ice cream, fruits, candies, piñatas, and more. A party begins; meanwhile, from behind a screen, Shadow watches.

***

"Another celebration?! It can't be! So many parties. I hate parties! I hate so much sweetness. I hate that girl! Grrr!" Pounding on the screen, Shadow expresses his fury. Karen Amanda is overjoyed at the sight of so much happiness and, accompanied by Piloso, takes it upon herself to entertain the children. Yet, despite all the joy around her, the girl feels sad, because she does not feel that the happiness is truly growing inside her.

"This joy is not mine, the girl says."

"It's a borrowed joy... it prepares you for your own," Piloso explains.

"I don't feel like it's real happiness; I can't fake a smile, and besides, it just won't come out," the girl affirms, as she moves her mouth, trying to force a smile.

"You have to be patient; it's only a matter of time."

"You know, Pilo, I want to go back home!"

"Don't ask me that. Are you going to throw everything away when we're so close? You deserve to smile again; we really are close."

"Who says so?"

"I say so. Or do you doubt me? I've never been so sure of anything," Piloso says, very serious and convinced.

Karen Amanda falls into deep thought, immersed in a silence that neither the children nor Rosita notice.

"Open the whirlpool to my house, please!"

Piloso has no other choice. He draws a hole in the void. Through the whirlpool, the girl sees some other girls writing on the walls of the school bathroom.

"Don't do that! That's what notebooks are for!" Karen Amanda shouts at the girls, who, seeing her face suspended in the void, flee the bathroom screaming in terror.

Immediately, Grandpa Lorenzo's face appears in the whirlpool, smiling. She gets excited as a succession of images passes by, of those who are happy because of her help. Finally, the image of her mother appears.

"Why not?! I'm going to try one more time."

"What did you say...? I didn't hear you," Piloso asks.

"Let's keep going," the girl confirms excitedly. Piloso closes the whirlpool. He celebrates her decision by jumping around. Rosita approaches them, curious to know what is happening.

"We have to go; we're searching for happiness," the girl explains.

"I can give you some information. Over on that hill is the Tevecom station. I once took the children there on a field trip. Tevecom is very kind and transmits happiness to the whole world all the time," Rosita informs her new friends.

"That sounds exciting. Maybe he can help us," the girl says, a bright sparkle in her eyes.

"His name is Tevecom? Sounds like Nevecon to me," Piloso chimes in with a grin.

Karen Amanda and Piloso leave Rosita's Garden and head towards the television station. They move forward excitedly, hoping to find the long-awaited joy. The station has an infrastructure of concrete blocks, a helipad, powerful relay antennas, green areas, and more. They seek happiness, but they have no idea what awaits them. Shadow has taken possession of the kind-hearted Tevecom, and things won't be so easy for the visitors.

"CONTINUE, WELCOME, HAPPINESS IS AT THE END OF THE ROAD," can be heard through a screen programmed to repeat that message constantly.

"Listen, happiness, joy in abundance!" The girl says excitedly to Piloso.

"I hear it! I hear it, Karen!"

They continue walking until they reach a hallway where they find another screen, on which a cartoon character repeats the happiness message. The walls are filled with posters of worldwide film and television hits. After passing through the corridor, they enter a large room, which is very dark but brightens when a screen turns on, as if it were expecting them. On the screen, a character appears, whose voice begins to lure them in:

"Come closer. Don't be afraid. Come closer! Look into my eyes." It is a very convincing voice, and that is how Karen Amanda and Piloso fall under the spell of the television broadcast, mesmerized by the phrase repeated on all the monitors in the station:

"WELCOME, HAPPINESS IS AT THE END OF THE ROAD."

Now under Shadow's power, they do not realize that the lit-up screen is none other than Tevecom's head, attached to a body made up of a mass of cables and connections, ending in a larger connection, giving Tevecom the appearance of having a tail. This major connection is unplugged but still operates through Shadow's power. Tevecom sits while the visitors remain hypnotized by his screen. Shadow projects a selection of the saddest and most painful scenes ever seen in film and television; immediately, Karen Amanda begins to age, and Piloso bursts into inconsolable tears.

"This time, you won't escape. I see you crying!" Shadow celebrates in triumph, but before she can finish speaking, the spirit of the grandfather, sensing his granddaughter's suffering, arrives and enters through Tevecom's major connection. The grandfather's spirit begins to interfere with the broadcast, slipping in occasional happy images, which Shadow desperately tries to block.

"This can't be! What is this?!" Shadow screams.

The happy images from the grandfather keep increasing, memories of his life with Karen Amanda.

"Stop it! Stop it! This can't be happening! No!" Shadow rages.

With the intervention of the grandfather's spirit, the girl begins to grow young again until she returns to being a normal child, her backpack on her back. Piloso is overjoyed; his tears dry up. At last, the screen fills with the grandfather's smiling face, zooming in on his grin, reaching the girl's eyes, and at that moment, filled with emotion, she smiles from the heart.

Karen Amanda and Piloso jump up, awakened by the new sensation. She is overflowing with joy. She spins, tosses her hair in the air, raises her arms, hugs Piloso, and smiles once more. She is as happy as when her grandfather used to read her bedtime stories.

Shadow, seeing her smile, grows even more furious; the screen shuts off, plunging the room into darkness. Under Shadow's control, Tevecom rises, turns the screen back on, and threatens:

"All your effort was for nothing; I invite you to watch this."

Without hesitation, Shadow projects onto the screen the suffering and tears of the children in the eternal games, General Star, the BullFrog family, Kalkuleitor, and Rosita, all facing impossible trials.

"Are you willing to sacrifice them for nothing? For your fake smile? That thing with your grandfather was just a television illusion," Shadow declares, convinced she has broken the girl's spirit.

"That's a lie... it may have been an illusion, but what I feel now is real, from the heart, and no one can take it away from me," the girl replies, throwing the portable hole at her.

"Pathetic gadgets! I laugh in your face," Shadow sneers, dodging the attack. Without hesitation, the girl blows her whistle with all her might.

"If you can't think about me because you're so happy, then think about your dear Pilosín!" Shadow commands. Piloso falls to the ground, clutching his head, as if it were about to explode.

"Stop blowing it, please, Karona!" Piloso begs.

The girl stops blowing and whispers to Piloso, asking him to create a special weapon. Piloso draws and instantly materializes a super gun, which the girl eagerly takes in her hands, kisses, and fires at Shadow. The shot lands on Tevecom's controlled arm, causing him to feel a slight sensation of joy.

"What do you think? This beauty shoots smiles!" Karen Amanda proudly exclaims, showing off the gun to Shadow, who flees into another room in the station.

"I think he smiled!" The girl tells Piloso.

"Bravo!" Piloso cheers excitedly.

Shadow is terrified by the girl's attack. Inside a supply room, hidden among cardboard boxes, Shadow tends to the wound left by that touch of happiness. He raises his hands, chants incantations, and a surge of electricity materializes La Llorona, La Patasola, the Hairy Hand, and El Mohan.

The terror these creatures evoke seeps through the station's connections, spreading through a macabre melody projected on the screens.

"Go! Find that girl and terrify her; scare her so much that she cries!" Shadow orders the creatures, who immediately set out in search of Karen Amanda and Piloso, now alerted by the eerie music, they prepare to face them in the building's corridors. A dense fog engulfs everything. The creatures wail and moan, trying to frighten them, but the girl remains calm.

"Do you happen to know them? I don't have the pleasure," Piloso admits, frightened.

"I'll tell you, this woman approaching is La Llorona... Llorona, don't cry anymore, your child has been found, he is on heaven's list. He's an angel! Of course, many Lloronas remain, because their children are still missing... too many missing..."

Upon hearing the truth, La Llorona dissolves into the mist, leaving behind an aura of colors far greater than a rainbow. Immediately, La Patasola rushes to kick Piloso, but the girl steps in her way.

"And you, Patasola, from now on, you won't be alone anymore! Pilo! Please, draw her a sweetheart."

Piloso draws a foot for Patasola.

"But be careful with foot-trapping mines!" The girl warns.

The two feet touch their toes, fall in love, and vanish, leaving behind a trail of glowing hearts that clear part of the fog. Piloso shudders nervously and touches something on his head. It's The Hairy Hand, clinging to his red eraser.

"Karona, what a hairy hand you have!" says Pilo, thinking it belongs to the girl.

"That's not my hand. That's The Hairy Hand," the girl replies with a smile.

"Yikes! What is this? What do we do with this hairy thing?" The Hairy Hand's hairs stand on end, and it tries to hide.

"Under all that fur, there's a beautiful hand. Let me shave you," the girl says sweetly.

Piloso draws a razor, a chair just the right size for the hand, and, applying menthol shaving foam, shaves The hairy Hand, which fades away, leaving behind a fresh, clean scent.

"One left. I'm exhausted," Piloso sighs.

"Leave this one to me... Mister Mohan, please." At the girl's request, the Mohan lets out a terrible howl, flails his small body, and reveals claw-like nails. The girl approaches slowly, his howling and wild movements diminishing until she gets close enough to kiss him on the head. Instantly, El Mohan disappears, taking the last remnants of fog with him. Karen Amanda and Piloso embrace, celebrating another victory. Their triumphant music plays across the screens, letting Shadow know of yet another failure.

"Failures! Even a gelatin wouldn't tremble at those pitiful wails! I summon! By the power I conjure, terrible gunmen shall appear!" Shadow, still recovering in her chamber from the smile that wounded his arm.

Rages as she summons two fearsome gunslingers. One from a modern city, the other from the Wild West. Both armed to the teeth, ready to defend their reputation as destroyers. Shadow sets the stage, filling the air with tense silence and ominous music.

Karen Amanda and Piloso sense the shift in atmosphere, stop celebrating, and brace themselves for a new, greater danger. The gunmen attack, firing their sad faces, bullets of sorrow from their weapons, straight at Karen Amanda and Piloso, who race through the station's hallways. A blast of sadness hits Piloso in the chest as he throws himself in front of the girl to protect her. Piloso falls, making a pitiful expression:

"Ahhh! They got me..."

Seeing him wounded by sorrow, the girl quickly shoots him a smile, restoring his happiness.

They press on. Karen Amanda trades shots of smiles and sadness with one of the gunmen.

"Right in the heart!" the girl exclaims, smiling.

The gunman drops to his knees, a warm smile spreading across his face. His image dissolves, returning him to the Wild West. Witnessing this, the modern-day gunslinger launches a storm of sorrow, but Karen Amanda lands a perfect shot right on his mouth, drawing a smile upon him. He stumbles backward against a wall, vanishes, and reappears, grinning, back in the big city.

"You're amazing! Not a cold-blooded bone in your body!" Piloso exclaims in admiration.

The girl kisses the barrel of her gun, from which smoky smiles rise.

"That's me! Karen Amanda..." she says, grinning. Then she shouts: "Where are you!? Why won't you face me!? Are you scared...? I challenge you to a duel, right here!" Shadow can take no more. He finally steps forward, standing a few meters away from the girl, materializing a weapon.

"If that's what you want, I'll oblige."

"I will defeat you!" The girl declares with a smile.

"I'll count to three, then you may fire. One, two, three." Piloso finishes counting, but the only sound is the laughter filling Shadow's sorrowful heart. He has no chance to shoot. Instead, he begins to chuckle nervously, then bursts into uncontrollable laughter, to the girl's shot.

Seizing the moment, Piloso reconnects Tevecom's main connection, which was still free. Tevecom reactivates, but on its screen, the image of a sinister figure appears, cackling.

"When you least expect it, I shall return! Ha, ha, ha!"

Tevecom fully regains control of its broadcast, but appears confused.

"What happened? My circuits ache, and my channels feel scrambled." Piloso makes a request:

"Let me use the keyboard." Tevecom opens a compartment in his chest, revealing a computer keyboard. Karen Amanda takes the lead, checking to ensure smiles are still present in the world.

"Piloso, please, I want to see my mom."

Piloso draws a virtual window, which opens in a swirling vortex, leading to the girls' bathroom.

"Tevecom, take care of the programming. We've left it free of sadness." The girl steps through the window. Piloso closes the vortex, and shrinks back himself to the size of a normal pencil. She tucks it into her backpack and walks out of the girls' bathroom, emerging into the school hallway, just as the school day ends. At the front entrance, her mother is waiting.

Karen Amanda runs to her, smiling, and they embrace.

www.ingramcontent.com/pod-product-compliance
Lightning Source LLC
LaVergne TN
LVHW041546070526
838199LV00046B/1853